Tundra Books, a division of Random House of Canada Limited, a Penguin Random House Company

Library and Archives Canada Cataloguing in Publication

Takeuchi, Chihiro, author
       Can you find my robot's arm? / Chihiro Takeuchi.
Issued in print and electronic formats.
ISBN 978-1-101-91903-3 (hardback).—ISBN 978-1-101-91904-0 (epub)
       I. Title.
PZ7.1.T35Ca 2017   j823'.92   C2016-905234-6
                                                    C2016-905235-4

Published simultaneously in the United States of America by Tundra Books of Northern New York, a division of Random House of Canada Limited, a Penguin Random House Company

Originally published in 2016 by Berbay Publishing Pty Ltd, Victoria, Australia

Library of Congress Control Number: 2016948353

North American edition edited by Peter Phillips
Designed by John Canty Design
The text was set in Futura.

Printed and bound in China

www.penguinrandomhouse.ca

1   2   3   4   5   21   20   19   18   17

Can you find

my robot's arm?

Chihiro Takeuchi

TUNDRA BOOKS

One morning, my robot woke up to discover he had lost his arm.

We searched the house,

but my robot's arm was nowhere to be found.

No, a fork will not do as a robot arm.

No, a broom won't make a good arm.

Neither will a pencil.

Neither will scissors.

And an umbrella certainly won't do.

Let's look outside.

It's not up in the tree.

Will this fallen branch do?

It isn't in the garden,

but will this leaf do?

It isn't in the amusement park,

but will this lollipop do?

How about this fish bone?

No way!

Would you like to try this arm on?

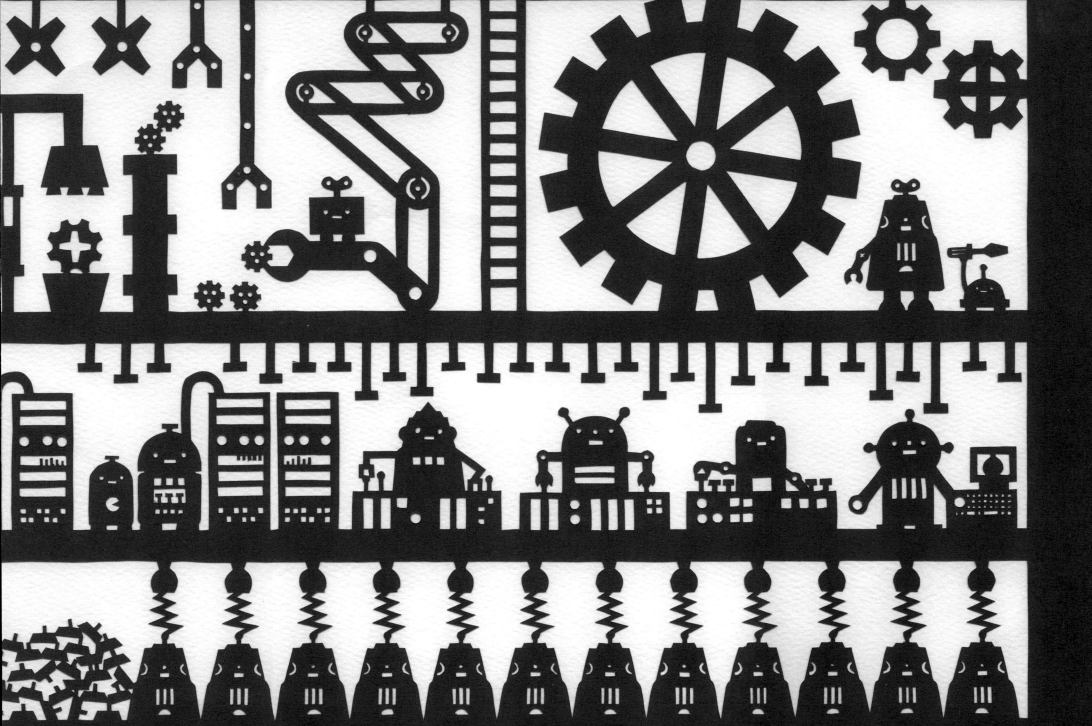

Nope, it's not up here either.

How about this robot arm?

Shall we look in here?

Sweet!

We can't find my robot's arm anywhere.

Let's go home.

Oh well. Maybe a fork is not such a bad arm after all.